PARTY!

by Diana G. Gallagher

illustrated by Brann Garvey

Librarian Reviewer
Laurie K. Holland
Media Specialist (National Board Certified), Edina, MN
MA in Elementary Education, Minnesota State University, Mankato

Reading Consultant
Sherry Klehr
Elementary/Middle School Educator, Edina Public Schools, MN
MA in Education, University of Minnesota

Claudia Cristina Cortez is published by Stone Arch Books,
A Capstone Imprint
151 Good Counsel Drive, P.O. Box 669
Mankato, Minnesota 56002
www.capstonepub.com

Copyright © 2009 by Stone Arch Books

Library of Congress Cataloging-in-Publication Data
Gallagher, Diana G.
    Party!: The Complicated Life of Claudia Cristina Cortez / by Diana G.
Gallagher; illustrated by Brann Garvey.
    p. cm. — (Claudia Cristina Cortez)
    ISBN 978-1-4342-0771-5 (library binding)
    ISBN 978-1-4342-0867-5 (pbk.)
    [1. Parties—Fiction. 2. Interpersonal relations—Fiction. 3. Middle
schools—Fiction. 4. Schools—Fiction.] I. Garvey, Brann, ill. II. Title.
PZ7.G13543Par 2009
[Fic]—dc21   2008004286

Summary: Claudia is throwing a party, but she has to save money to pay for it.
She's spending all of her time working, and neglecting her friends. What good is a
party with no one to invite to it?

Art Director: Heather Kindseth
Graphic Designer: Kay Fraser

Photo Credits
Delaney Photography, cover, 1

Printed in the United States of America in Stevens Point, Wisconsin.
092010
005957R

Table of Contents

Cast of

ME

CLAUDIA
That's me. I'm thirteen, and I'm in the seventh grade at Pine Tree Middle School. I live with my mom, my dad, and my brother, Jimmy. I have one cat, Ping-Ping. I like music, baseball, and hanging out with my friends.

MONICA is my very best friend. We met when we were really little, and we've been best friends ever since. I don't know what I'd do without her! Monica loves horses. In fact, when she grows up, she wants to be an Olympic rider!

MONICA

BECCA

BECCA is one of my closest friends. She lives next door to Monica. Becca is really, really smart. She gets good grades. She's also really good at art.

ADAM and I met when we were in third grade. Now that we're teenagers, we don't spend as much time together as we did when we were kids, but he's always there for me when I need him. (Plus, he's the only person who wants to talk about baseball with me!)

ADAM

Characters

TOMMY's our class clown. Sometimes he's really funny, but sometimes he is just annoying. Becca has a crush on him . . . but I'd never tell.

I think **PETER** is probably the smartest person I've ever met. Seriously. He's even smarter than our teachers! He's also one of my friends. Which is lucky, because sometimes he helps me with homework.

Every school has a bully, and **JENNY** is ours. She's the tallest person in our class, and the meanest, too. She always threatens to stomp people. No one's ever seen her stomp anyone, but that doesn't mean it hasn't happened!

ANNA is the most popular girl at our school. Everyone wants to be friends with her. I think that's weird, because Anna can be really, really mean. I mostly try to stay away from her.

Cast of

CARLY is Anna's best friend. She always tries to act exactly like Anna does. She even wears the exact same clothes. She's never really been mean to me, but she's never been nice to me either!

NICK is my annoying seven-year-old neighbor. I get stuck babysitting him a lot. He likes to make me miserable. (Okay, he's not that bad ALL of the time . . . just most of the time.)

SYLVIA really wants to be one of Anna's friends, but Anna doesn't act very nice to her. In fact, sometimes it seems like Anna doesn't like Sylvia at all. I don't mind Sylvia, but I wish she didn't care so much about trying to impress Anna.

Characters

JIMMY is my big brother. I stay out of his way, and he stays out of mine.

JIMMY

MOM

My **MOM** and **DAD** are pretty good parents. They give good advice, most of the time, but sometimes I wish they'd just let me do my own thing!

DAD

UNCLE DIEGO

UNCLE DIEGO is my dad's brother. He hangs out at our house a lot. I really like him because he treats me like an adult. Also, he tells funny jokes.

CHAPTER 1

Popular Party

Being one of the cool kids is not on the **Claudia Cristina Cortez Wish List.**

For one reason: **Anna Dunlap.**

Why?

Because Anna is the boss of:

1. All of her friends

2. The seventh grade at Pine Tree Middle School

And she isn't nice about it.

Anna is:

1. Popular

2. Stuck up

3. Bossy

A lot of girls try to be Anna's friends. They think that being friends with the school's most popular girl will make them popular too.

I have *five really close friends,* and I get along with most people. That is popular enough for me.

But every now and then I get **jealous,** and I wish that I was **popular** too.

When you're popular, you do things that everyone else talks about. For example, when I have a party, **no one else in the seventh grade cares,** except for my five friends. But when Anna has a party, she invites a ton of people and *everyone* talks about it.

Anna was having a big beach party on Saturday. It was the only thing we talked about at lunch.

"Anna's party makes me miss fifth grade," **Monica** said.

"It does?" Becca asked. She looked confused.

"Everybody was invited to everybody's parties in elementary school," Monica explained.

"Even Jenny Pinski," **Adam** said.

"It doesn't work that way in middle school," Monica went on. **"The cool kids only invite other cool kids."**

"We get the cold shoulder," **Tommy** said. "Then the cool crowd chills out together."

Some of Tommy's jokes were HILARIOUS. Nobody laughed at that one. Being left out isn't funny when you're thirteen.

But nobody wanted to admit they cared. Everyone tried to act like they didn't want to go to the party anyway.

"I couldn't go to a party this Saturday anyway," Monica said. "I have a **horseback riding** lesson."

Monica would skip one lesson to go to a beach party.

"I have a **baseball game**," Adam said.

Anna's party started at three. The game would be over by then.

"I hate *sand in my shoes*," Becca said. "And getting **sunburned.** And the lake bottom is YUCKY."

Becca could go barefoot, use sunscreen, and float.

"Lake muck is neat," Tommy said. "It squishes between your toes like SLIME."

"Right. YUCK," Becca said, making a face.

"I don't swim very well," Peter said.

A lot of kids didn't go in the water even when they went to a beach party. Anna's friends probably wouldn't go into the water because they didn't want to mess up **their perfect hair.**

I love the lake. I don't mind **sand** in my shoes, **muck** between my toes, or getting my hair WET. I like **diving for rocks** and looking for **turtles.** I also like hanging out with my friends. Anna's beach party would be a blast if I could go with all of my friends.

But my friends and I weren't invited.

CHAPTER 2

Bad Beach Day

Saturday was the day of Anna's party. It was also the day of the **Cortez Computers Company Picnic.** My dad owns a computer store, and every year, he has a party for his employees. The store closes early so everyone can come. They bring their families. My dad brings the food.

The Cortez Computers Picnic Guest List

Dad, Mom, Jimmy (16), Claudia (13)

Uncle Diego

Mr. & Mrs. Drake, Carson (5), Kari (2)

Simon Fitch (college guy computer genius)

Nick Wright (7)

Nick doesn't work at the store. He's the **pint-sized pest** that lives next door. My mom watches him at our house when his parents are busy. Even though Nick doesn't work at the computer store and he's not in our family, he's never missed a store picnic.

Mom says we should just **adopt** Nick, but I told her I'd have to move out if that happened. **Nobody can handle Nick 24/7.**

Uncle Diego doesn't work at the store either, but he comes to the picnic every year anyway. He brings the **potato salad.**

The store picnic is usually fun. **But we don't usually have it:**

1. At the lake
2. On the same day Anna has a beach party I'm not invited to.

Anna's party had already started when we got to the lake on Saturday afternoon. Music was blaring from a *BOOM BOX*.

Anna's dad was cooking *hamburgers* on a grill. Her mom was handing out *sodas* and *chips.* Kids were swimming, eating, and playing volleyball. Some of them were dancing.

Everyone looked like they were having a great time.

Brad Turino, the guy I have a crush on (but no one knows), was there too. He was wearing baggy beach shorts. His white shirt was flapping in the breeze. He was talking to **Anna**, who was wearing a pink bikini. They looked 𝒞𝒪𝒪𝐿, like California surfers in a movie or something.

I pretended not to notice. I hoped Brad and Anna didn't notice me.

I looked like a **dorky mother duck** as I walked down the beach toward the Cortez Computers sign at our picnic spot. Three noisy little kids walked behind me: Nick, Carson, and Kari. And I was carrying a purple swim ring and a Bonk-o bat.

Of course, that's when Anna and Carly noticed me. "Hey, Claudia!" Anna yelled. "Where's your **pail and shovel?**"

"Claudia doesn't need a pail," Carly said, smirking. "She has a **pretty plastic swim ring.**"

Nick grabbed the bat out of my hands. Then he whacked me. "**BONK-O!**" he screamed.

Some of Anna's friends laughed.

Then I noticed that Brad was WAVING.
I couldn't tell who he was waving at. It almost seemed
like he was waving at me . . . but **what if he wasn't?** So
I didn't wave back. **I blushed and kept walking.**

I wanted to hide, but I couldn't. Our picnic area
was next to Anna's party. We had a little building for
our picnic, but it only had a roof. There were no sides
on the building. I could see everyone at Anna's party,
and they could see me. So something *humiliating* had
to happen.

And then it did. Nick dropped an ice cube down
my back. I squealed and jumped up. "Nick!" I yelled.

"Hey!" **Carly** yelled. "Look, everybody!
Claudia's doing some kind of **freaky dance!**"

I jiggled and wiggled until the ice cube fell
out of my shirt. Nick pointed and laughed. He
doubled over and laughed harder. Then he rolled
on the sand and laughed like a **maniac.**

Jimmy and Simon were sitting at the picnic table,
playing handheld video games.

Jimmy saw what was happening. He said, "Nick, want to play my game for a while?" Then Nick stopped laughing. He ran over and grabbed the game from Jimmy.

"Thanks," I said.

Jimmy shrugged. "Whatever," he said.

Then **Mom** ran up, looking frantic. "Claudia, can you watch Carson and Kari while Mrs. Drake and I set up our picnic?" she asked.

I shrugged. "Okay," I said. Two little kids couldn't be as much TROUBLE as Nick.

I looked at Carson and Kari, who were standing next to their mom. "Let's take a walk," I said.

Carson picked up his pail. "Let's find **frogs** and **snakes!**" he yelled.

"That sounds like a good plan," I told him. I only agreed because I knew he wouldn't find any. The beach was too crowded.

Carson was happy looking for rocks anyway. He was a pretty easy kid.

But Kari was a **problem.** Two-year-old girls do what they want. They don't listen, and they're even **more selfish than Anna is.**

While we were hunting for rocks, Kari noticed that another little girl had a purple swim ring just like hers. Kari saw it and went CRAZY!

"Mine!" Kari yelled. She took off.

"Kari, no!" I yelled. I took off after her. She was headed for the lake, and she couldn't swim.

Kari was fast for **a tiny kid with stubby legs.** I caught her just before her toes got wet. "There's your swim ring, Kari," I said, pointing at our beach toys, in a pile next to our picnic spot.

But Kari didn't care about her swim ring anymore. She wanted Carson's pail. "Mine!" she yelled. Then she took off again.

"Wait!" I yelled. I started to run after her, but I tripped over a rock and fell in the sand.

"You're supposed to dive into the water, not the sand, Claudia!" **Anna** shouted. A bunch of other kids laughed.

Suddenly, **two feet appeared right by my nose,** which was buried in the sand. "Are you okay?" a voice asked.

It was Brad!

I couldn't answer. I couldn't talk to Brad. I mean, I really couldn't talk to him. I always *stuttered or choked up.*

I just nodded. Brad helped me up. I mumbled, "Thanks." But I don't think he heard me.

"The **hamburgers** are ready, Brad!" Anna called out.

"See you later, Claudia," Brad said. Then he left.

My leg hurt. I was covered with sand. **My dignity was wrecked.** And Brad probably thought I was a clumsy idiot. **Could things get any worse?**

Carson handed me **a dead fish.** "Can we 𝔼𝔸𝕋 this?" he asked.

After I stopped gagging, I took Carson and Kari back to their mom. Mom told me to take a break. I grabbed Jimmy's inner tube and ran to the lake.

Nothing could make me feel better. But floating helped me RELAX.

I relaxed, that is, until Jimmy flipped the inner tube and dumped me in the water. Nick thought that was **hilarious.** He screamed, pointed, and laughed. So did everyone at Anna's party.

After I dried off, I sat by **Uncle Diego** at the picnic table. "I'm having one of those days where **I just can't win**," I said.

Uncle Diego nodded like he understood. "**Murphy's Law**," he said.

"What's that?" I asked. "Who's Murphy?"

"Murphy's Law says that **if something can go wrong, it will go wrong**," my uncle told me.

"Well, it could, and it did," I said sadly. "Everything that could possibly go wrong has. *This might be the worst day of my life.*"

CHAPTER 3

Revenge

I've done a lot of **embarrassing things** in my life.

A. I tried to sneak out of the backyard when I was six. My shorts got caught on the fence. The whole neighborhood heard me screaming. Mom found me **hanging from the fence** by the seat of my pants.

B. I let Monica cut my hair in fourth grade. Mom had to pay a real hairdresser to fix it. I looked like a 𝔹𝕆𝕐 for three months.

C. We had beef stew for lunch one day last year. It upset my stomach. I felt sick and ran for the rest room. But I ran into the boys' room by mistake! Everybody laughed when I came back out. Then I **threw up** on the floor in front of everyone.

Those were bad moments. But they weren't as bad as the day at the beach. Anna would tell everyone at school all of the embarrassing things that had happened to me. **My social life would be dead by lunch on Monday.**

I was so upset I called all of my friends on Sunday morning and asked them to come over.

I must have sounded **pretty sad** on the phone, because Monica, Becca, and Adam looked **WORRIED** when they got to my house.

"Are you mad at us?" **Becca** asked.

"No, I'm mad at Anna," I explained.

"Because she didn't invite us to her party?" **Adam** asked.

"Yes. I'm tired of being left out," I said.

"We can't make Anna invite us," Becca said.

"That's not the only thing I'm mad about," I admitted. Then I told them what happened at the lake.

"Anna laughed when you fell?" **Monica** whispered. She looked shocked. "That's **terrible**."

"Yes, it was," I agreed. "And **I want Anna to pay**."

"But getting **revenge** would make you just as bad as Anna," Becca said.

"I don't care," I said. And I meant it.

"You could put **worms in her backpack**,"
Adam suggested.

"Too gross," I said.

"You could throw an even cooler party and not
invite Anna," Monica said. **"That's the best way to
get back at her."**

* * *

I was still angry when I went to bed. I couldn't
sleep. I just kept thinking about REVENGE.

Revenge is sweet.

Cold revenge is better.

Don't get mad, get even.

I had to get even with Anna.

Not just for me. For everyone Anna has ever left
out, made fun of, or laughed at.

Monica's idea was a good one. That got me
thinking about having *a cool party*. But what would
beat a beach party?

I thought about it. A pool party at the **Community Center** would be ten times better than Anna's beach party. I'd invite **everyone** in the seventh grade except Anna and her friends.

It was a fantastic plan. Except for one thing. It costs money to rent the Community Center.

And I only had $32.57.

CHAPTER 4

Dad's Two Cents

Throwing a pool party was **a huge project.** I didn't know where to start. The next morning, I went to talk to my dad.

"I need some **advice,** Dad," I said.

Dad lowered his newspaper. "Are you in TROUBLE?" he asked.

"Well, kind of. I want to rent the **party room** at the Community Center," I explained. "The one with the pool."

"Why?" Dad asked.

I couldn't tell him the real reason. **He doesn't like the idea of getting even.**

I thought about it. Then I said, "I want to do something nice for my friends." That was **the truth.** It just wasn't *the whole truth.*

Dad thought about that for a minute. Then he asked a bunch of questions.

Dad's Questions and My Answers
(And What I Thought)

Dad: How much will the party room cost?

Me: I don't know.

I did know it was more than I had.

Dad: When do you want to have this party?

Me: A week from next Saturday.

Dad: Are you having refreshments?

Me: Yes.

I didn't know what to serve, but it would be something better than hamburgers, soda, and chips!

Dad: You'll need adult chaperones. Who are you going to ask?

Me: You and Mom?

Who else would I ask?

Dad: How are you going to pay for everything?

Me: I'll do chores for the neighbors, babysit Nick, and I have some money saved.

I found a nickel under my bed. $32.62 wasn't enough, but it was a start.

"Well, you'd better get BUSY," Dad said.

He was right about that! First I had to find out about the pool-and-party room.

"I'll go to the **Community Center** after school," I said.

Dad nodded and went back to reading his newspaper. I headed back to my room to get ready for school.

Uncle Diego stopped me in the hall. "Planning a party?" he asked.

"The best party ever," I said.

"Don't forget Murphy's Law," Uncle Diego warned.

Party Plan

I went to the Community Center after school. It is a big, new building a few blocks away from my school.

When I walked in the front door, I saw another door marked **RENTAL OFFICE.** I went in.

A woman was sitting at a desk. She looked up when I opened the door. "Can I help you?" she asked.

I took a deep breath. "I would like to rent a party room," I said. "The one with the pool."

"All right," the woman said. I noticed that she had a badge clipped to her shirt. **It said Janet.**

"Why don't you have a seat," Janet said. "I have some paperwork we'll need to fill out."

I sat down in a chair across from her. Janet rummaged through a drawer and pulled out a stack of papers. "All right," she said. "Let's get started. Name?"

"**Claudia Cortez,**" I told her.

"And when would you like to rent the room, Claudia?" Janet asked.

"*A week from Saturday,*" I said. "Starting at 6 p.m."

Janet looked at a big calendar on her desk. Then she wrote my name in one of the squares. **"You're in luck!"** she said. "The pool room is open that day."

"Great!" I said.

"Now, how many people are you inviting? You'll need to have **one adult chaperone for every 20 kids,**" she told me.

"I'm inviting **75 people,**" I said. "So I guess I need four chaperones."

Janet smiled. "That's right. Would you like the Community Center to provide the **food and drinks?**"

"Is that **EXTRA?**" I asked.

"It is," Janet told me. "It's an extra **hundred dollars.** We'll need half of that money this Saturday. That's **not refundable** if you cancel the party."

"Okay," I said slowly.

Saturday was really soon. I wasn't sure I could make fifty dollars that fast. But **I had to try.** "How much does it cost to rent the room?" I asked.

Janet looked at a piece of paper on her desk. "It's **one hundred dollars,**" she told me. "And again, we'll need the first half by Saturday."

"So I need to pay you **one hundred dollars total** on Saturday?" I asked. This party was going to cost way more than I thought!

"That's right. Will that work for you, Claudia?" she asked.

"Yes," I said. I sighed. It wasn't going to be easy. **But once Claudia Cortez has a plan, she sticks to it!**

* * *

Okay, so **I didn't really have a plan.** After I got home from the Community Center, I went to the tree house in my back yard to work on my project.

But then **Nick** found me in the tree house.

"What are you doing, Claudia?" Nick asked.

"Making a list," I said.

First Mistake: I should have said, "Doing my homework." Nick would have thought that was boring and gone away.

"A list of what?" Nick asked. He tried to look at my notebook.

"It's a SECRET," I told him, covering my notes with my hand.

Second Mistake: I should have said, "School supplies." Secrets just make Nick more curious.

"I won't tell," Nick said.

"I know you won't," I said. "Because **I won't tell you.**"

Even my friends didn't know about the pool party. I wanted it to be a SURPRISE when I passed out invitations.

"If you don't tell me, I'll make you **sorry**," Nick growled.

He glared at me. **He wasn't kidding.**

Nick will do anything to get what he wants. He'll
LIE, **KICK**, and **BREAK** things. And that's just
for starters.

It would be easier to give in before Nick did
something awful. Then I'd have to give in anyway.

"It's a surprise," I said. "You can't tell anyone."
I held out my pinky finger and said, **"Pinky promise."**

Nick hooked his pinky around mine. "Promise,"
he said.

"I'm throwing a pool party for my friends," I said.

**Third Mistake: I should have said, "I'm doing chores
for Mom." Nick would not want to help.**

Nick's eyes got big. "Can I come?" he asked.

"No. Seventh graders only," I said.

Nick frowned. He stuck out his chin and folded
his arms. He whispered, "If you don't let me come, **I'll
make you really sorry.**" Then he just stared angrily
at me.

Biggest Mistake: Forgetting Murphy's Law.

I stared back at Nick.

I knew one thing for sure. There was no way Nick was going to my pool party. **But he didn't have to know that yet.**

"I'll think about it," I said.

"You will?" Nick asked.

"Yes, I will," I told him. That wasn't exactly a lie. I would think about it. I'd think about all the reasons Nick couldn't come. "Now go away so I can finish my list," I said.

Nick left. Then I wrote down everything I needed.

Pool Party Plan

1. Community Center

>   Rented for a week from Saturday.

>   Cost = $100

> $50.00 deposit by this Saturday

> $50.00 more on party day

>   Deposit not returned if I cancel

2. Food: Community Center refreshments = $100

> $50 deposit on Saturday

3. Chaperones (4 chaperones needed)

Ask: Mom & Dad, Mr. & Mrs. Gomez

4. Music

Something better than CDs
on a boom box

Or a D. J.

Or a real band (I can dream, can't I?)

5. Money: $200 needed

Find more jobs to do in the
neighborhood

Babysit Nick more (that should be worth $200
on its own . . . but it won't pay that much)

CHAPTER 6

Party, Inc.

I asked my usual customers if they knew anyone else who needed help. They all did. My business boomed.

On Thursday, I had to walk dogs after school. Plus, I was babysitting Nick.

Dog Walking

1. Buster (Mrs. Arnold's big, brown mutt)

2. Fancy (Mrs. Gomez's little poodle)

3. Corky (Mrs. Oliver's beagle)

4. Bob (Mr. Jones's small, black mutt)

It wasn't easy. I didn't have time to go around the block twice. I had to walk all four dogs at the same time. I picked up Fancy, then Buster, then Corky. I still had to get Bob, but I needed more hands!

Well, Nick had two hands. So I guess it was a good thing that Mom sent him on the walk with me.

"You can walk Fancy and Buster," I told Nick.

"**No,**" Nick said. He frowned and shoved his hands in his pockets.

"What?" I said, surprised. "You're always 𝔹𝕌𝔾𝔾𝕀ℕ𝔾 me to let you walk a dog!"

"Can I come to your pool party?" Nick asked.

I almost blurted out, "No." Then I remembered that **I'd promised to think about it.** "I haven't decided yet," I told him.

"Then **walk your own dumb dogs,**" Nick said. He turned his back.

I had to pay the **fifty-dollar deposit** in two days. I couldn't afford to lose customers. Plus, I'd promised to walk all the dogs by 4 p.m.

I made a deal with Nick. Bribery always works with him.

"I'll pay you **two dollars,**" I said. The two dollars Mom was paying me to watch him. That would mean I wouldn't get that two dollars, but **my dog-walking customers wouldn't be disappointed.**

"Okay," Nick said. He took Fancy and Buster's leashes.

It was the WORST dog walk ever.

Buster wrapped his leash around Nick's legs five times! Every time, Nick screeched, "**Stop it, Buster! Stop it!**"

Fancy whined until I picked her up. Then she WHINED if I tried to put her down, so I carried her.

Corky chased a cat and almost got away.

Bob barked at everything. Even **bugs.**

It was horrible.

Babysitting

I had a new babysitting customer. I had to be at the Mitchell house at 4 p.m.

Mikey Mitchell is ten months old. I had never watched a BABY before. But Mrs. Mitchell was only going to her neighbor's house for an hour or so.

Note: Babies are disgusting.

I had to feed Mikey a snack. His mom said he likes oatmeal. He doesn't. Every time I put some in his mouth, Mikey spit it out. **It wasn't fun.**

After babies eat, they usually need their diapers changed. **That part is definitely not fun.**

Changing Mikey's diaper wasn't easy. He flipped onto his stomach and tried to crawl away. He thought it was funny.

Note: You can't put a diaper on a baby if you're holding onto one of its feet.

Then I thought Mikey should sleep. But he did not want to take a nap. He started to doze off when I held him, but he SCREAMED when I put him in his crib. After three tries, I gave up.

We watched cartoons until his mom got home.

Conclusions:

A. Watching babies is worth more than $5.00 an hour.

B. Watching Nick is fun compared to watching babies.

Yard Work

After babysitting, it was already 5 p.m. I was scheduled for yard work at Mrs. Pike's house. Mr. Gomez was in his yard when I left the Mitchells' house.

"Why are you working so hard, Claudia?" **Mr. Gomez** asked.

"I'm having a PARTY," I explained. "At the Community Center."

"I rented the pool-and-party room last year," Mr. Gomez said. "We had a family reunion. **$300 is a lot of money.**"

"I only have to pay **$100,**" I said. "And another $100 for snacks."

"I guess you got the **kid price,**" Mr. Gomez said. "Well, good luck! Tell Mrs. Pike I said hello."

"I will," I said.

I headed to Mrs. Pike's house. Mr. Gomez had told her about me. Her flower gardens were full of **weeds,** and she needed help pulling them.

An Unexplained Law Of The Universe: Plants you don't want (weeds) grow better than plants you do want (flowers).

I weeded one of the gardens by Mrs. Pike's driveway. I didn't have time to weed both sides. Mrs. Pike said I could do it on Saturday. **She was happy with my work.**

I was **dirty, tired, hungry**, and a little WORRIED. After everyone paid me the next day, and I gave Nick his two dollars, I'd only have $91.32. I needed $100 for deposits on Saturday.

I was $8.68 short.

Only **one good thing** happened on Saturday. Jimmy let me help him mow lawns. He mowed. I trimmed around the walks.

The weed-eating tool made me NERVOUS, so I used clippers. It took forever. My back hurt afterward, but Jimmy paid me $10.

Then I paid the Community Center. I gave them $100. I couldn't get it back if I canceled the party. But **I wouldn't cancel the party unless:**

1. I got poison ivy from Mrs. Pike's garden.

2. The Community Center burned down.

3. Nobody wanted to come.

After that, I still had to earn another **$100.** I had a lot of work to do. I went home to change before I went to work. I didn't want **dog drool** or **dirt** on my good clothes. **Mom** and **Dad** stopped me in the kitchen.

"You FORGOT to fold the laundry,"
Mom said.

"Oops," I said. I *really had forgotten*. It was my
job to fold laundry every Saturday. I was just so busy
with other stuff, I forgot.

"Do your chores or no party," Dad said.

"I will," I promised. I went straight to the laundry
room. I folded FAST, but I was still **late** for dog
walking.

The last walk had been awful, so I decided not to
walk all four dogs at once. I took Buster and Fancy
around the block first. I carried the poodle so I could
walk faster. Buster doesn't mind **running** to keep up.

After I brought Buster and Fancy back to
their houses, I picked up Mrs. Oliver's beagle,
Corky. She stopped to sniff every mailbox, so
I was really late getting to Bob's house.
Mr. Jones had already taken Bob for a walk.

"**I'm sorry**, Mr. Jones," I said. "Please don't fire me."

"I won't," Mr. Jones said. "But I'm not going to pay
you for today."

That was fair. I didn't want money for work I didn't do.

By the end of the day, Mrs. Pike's gardens were **weed—free.** She was **really happy,** but she said she only needed me on Friday next week.

Money Coming In & Going Out

When I got home, I sat down to figure out my profits and expenses.

Profits = money I made

Expenses = money I lost

Profits:

Dog Walking: + $60.00

Mrs. Pike: + $ 5.00

Mr. Gomez: + $ 5.00

Babysitting Nick: + $10.00

Total Profits: $80

Expenses:

- $2.00 (missed Bob's walk)

- $6.00 (bribes)

Total Expenses: $8.00

$80 - $6 = $72.00

That wasn't enough. I had to find more dogs to walk, weeds to pull, or babies to watch. I still owed the Community Center **$100.** I needed **$28.00** . . . or there would be no party.

CHAPTER 8

Party Problems

Money wasn't my only problem. I still needed music. I had a boom box and CDs, and my MP3 player. **I wanted something better.**

My brother was a DJ at one of his school dances last year. I decided I'd ask him if he would DJ at my party. After all, **I had nothing to lose.**

Jimmy was in his room. He hates it when I go into his room without asking first. But if I ask to come in, he says, "**NO.**" So I don't ask.

The Jimmy/Claudia Problem

1. Jimmy hardly ever talks to me.

2. I almost never do what he says.

I walked into Jimmy's room without knocking.

"**Go away,**" Jimmy said.

"I need a favor," I told him.

"I'm **BUSY,**" Jimmy said. He didn't look at me. He just kept his eyes on his computer screen.

"Will you D.J. my pool party?" I asked.

"How much will you pay me?" Jimmy asked. He didn't stop playing.

"I can't pay you," I said. "That's why it's a **favor.**"

"Then I can't do it," Jimmy said. "Now go away."

I'd have to settle for a boom box like Anna had at her beach party. That wasn't as COOL as a D.J., but it wasn't TERRIBLE.

I went into my room and noticed a piece of paper lying on the floor. It was the **receipt** from my deposit at the Community Center.

I picked it up and looked closely at it. **I gasped when I read it.** The Community Center charged me $100 for snacks. But the receipt said I was only getting chips, pretzels, and sodas!

First I was *shocked.*

Next I got **mad.**

Then I did the **math.** 75 kids, 4 chaperones, and me added up to 80 people. That meant I was paying $1.25 per person for snacks. That was fair. But Anna's hamburgers were *better.*

Uncle Diego had warned me about Murphy's Law. **A lot of little things were going wrong.** I was just glad it wasn't worse.

An Unexplained Law of the Universe: Whenever you think or say, "Things could be worse," they get worse.

Before bed, my mom said I had a phone call. It was Monica. **She was mad at me.**

"I can't believe you missed the movie," she said.

I couldn't believe it either. Becca, Monica, and I have been planning to see **Super Hero High** for a month.

"We waited outside the theater until the last minute," **Monica** went on. "We almost missed the beginning, and we didn't have time to buy popcorn." I could tell she was *really upset*.

"I'm really sorry, Monica," I said.

"Where were you?" **Monica** asked.

"I *forgot*," I said quietly.

"You forgot?" Monica yelled. Then she said, "I have to go." Then she hung up.

Adam called ten seconds later. "Why didn't you come to the game today?" he asked. He sounded mad too.

Oh no! I **forgot** all about Adam's baseball game!

"I hit a home run, and **you missed it**," Adam said.

I felt terrible.

My three best friends were mad at me.

My pool party wouldn't be much fun if I didn't have any friends left to invite.

CHAPTER 9

Work and Worry

On Sunday, I was *TIRED,* so I slept late. Then I spent all day doing homework and chores. I fell asleep right after dinner.

None of my friends called me, and I didn't call them.

* * *

Monday started off pretty *BAD* too.

"What's going on?" **Becca** asked me in homeroom. "What happened on Saturday?"

"Nothing," I lied. **"I just forgot.** I'm really, really sorry."

"I don't understand how you forgot," Becca said sadly. "We planned the movie for **weeks.**"

I wanted to make up with my friends. But I couldn't tell them about the party. Not just because it would **spoil the surprise.**

I needed to make sure I could pay for the party first.

Question: What's the worst thing that could happen?

Answer: Having to cancel the party after everyone was invited.

Nobody knew about the party yet, so if I canceled it now, it wouldn't be a disappointment. But if I had to cancel after I invited everyone, the whole seventh grade would be mad at me.

No one would forget. Not for a gazillion years. **Anna** would make sure of that.

"You're acting WEIRD," Monica said.

"I am?" I asked. I tried to look puzzled.

"We hardly saw you at all last week," Becca said. "Except at school."

"You missed my home run," Adam said.

"I had stuff to do," I said. But I knew it was a lame excuse.

"Like what?" Monica asked.

"Just stuff," I answered.

Luckily, the bell rang then. I left before they asked more questions I couldn't answer.

Then I tried to **avoid them** for the rest of the day.

* * *

On Tuesday, I almost gave up.

Monica and Becca came to the **tree house** after school. They each brought copies of the magazines they'd gotten over the past month. We always got together once a month to share and read our magazines.

I had FORGOTTEN about that, too. Even though we always read our magazines on the first Tuesday of every month. I had dogs to walk.

"I can't stay," I said. I felt awful.

"Why not?" **Monica** asked. She looked confused and upset.

"I have to go somewhere," I explained.

"Claudia, don't you want to be friends anymore?" Becca asked sadly.

"Of course I do!" I said. I wanted to tell them everything, but **I didn't have time.** I couldn't be late to my dog-walking customers' houses.

"Let's go, Becca," Monica said. "Claudia has **more important things to do** than hang out with us."

Monica and Becca went away. They were 𝕊𝔸𝔻 and 𝕄𝔸𝔻.

Then Mom made me take **Nick** on my walk.

"Can I come to your pool party?" Nick asked while we walked to Bob's house.

I sighed. **Nick was the most annoying person I knew** — even worse than Anna. But it wasn't fair to keep fooling him.

"No," I said.

Nick kicked me.

I limped down the sidewalk. "Hurry up, Nick," I told him.

Nick didn't hurry up. He stopped to *tie his shoes.* That took five minutes. Finally, we made it to Bob's house.

We were running late, so I had to walk all four dogs at the same time again. **Nick wouldn't help.** And he wouldn't speed up until I bribed him.

We passed the park on the way home.

"I want to play on the 𝕊𝕎𝕀ℕ𝔾𝕊," Nick said.

"Not today," I told him. I really didn't have time. I had to babysit **Mikey** for an hour after dinner, and my homework wasn't done.

Nick stopped in the middle of the sidewalk. He crossed his arms and **glared** at me. Then he asked, "Can I come to your party?"

"No," I told him again.

Nick ran away.

I chased him around the playground for fifteen minutes. Nick finally got tired, but so did I.

That night at dinner, I fell asleep at the table.

Dad woke me up. "Claudia, this is **ridiculous,**" he said. "Go to your room and go to sleep."

"I can't," I told him. "I have to babysit Mikey."

Dad shook his head. "If you're falling asleep at the table, **you're too tired to babysit.** I want you to call Mrs. Mitchell and tell her you can't watch Mikey tonight. Then I want you to **cancel** the PARTY."

I gasped. "Dad!" I said. I could feel tears in my eyes, but I didn't cry. "I've been working so hard for the party. **Please don't make me cancel it.** Please. I can do it. I promise."

Dad looked at me for a minute. Finally he said, "Okay, Claudia. **One more chance.**"

But I wasn't sure I could do it.

CHAPTER 10

Spoiled and Saved

On Wednesday, I invited Monica, Becca, and Adam over after school.

When they came over, we went up to the **tree house** in my back yard. They sat on the bench and waited for me to start.

"Well, you guys are right," I began. "**I have been acting weird.** But there's a reason."

"Good," **Adam** said. "We don't want to be **MAD** at you." Monica and Becca nodded.

I took a deep breath. Then I told them **everything.**

"I was so **MAD** at Anna for not inviting us to her beach party and **making fun of me,**" I explained. "I had to do something, so I decided to throw a pool party for everyone except Anna and her friends. I've been working day and night to pay the Community Center. I wanted to tell you, but I couldn't, because **I wanted it to be a surprise.**"

"A party? **COOL!**" Adam exclaimed, grinning.

Monica and Becca looked down. They didn't smile.

"Are you still MAD?" I asked.

"No," Monica said. "I feel like a **jerk.**"

"Me too," Becca said. "We should have known you wouldn't **dump us.**"

"When is the party?" **Adam** asked.

"Saturday," I said. "If I don't have to cancel it," I added.

"Why would you have to cancel it?" Monica asked.

"I owe the Community Center **$100** for the room and some lame refreshments," I said. "I made $5.00 babysitting last night, but I'm still **$23.00 short.**"

Monica dug in her pocket and pulled out some crumpled money. "I'll chip in **$7.00,**" she said.

"I've got **$12.00,**" Adam said.

"I can give you **$4.00** at school tomorrow," Becca added, smiling. "That makes **$23.00.**"

"How *lame* are the refreshments?" Monica asked.

"Lame," I told her. "Pretzels, chips, soda."

Becca made a face. **"I can get more goodies,"** she said. "The Cooking Club will help."

"Just don't tell anyone at school until I pass out invitations," I said. "The party is still a **surprise**."

"Do we need anything else?" Adam asked.

"A D.J.," I said.

Adam smiled. "I'm your guy," he said. "I'll bring my MP3 player and speakers. **I have 10,000 songs."**

"I thought I could do everything myself," I said. "But I couldn't. Thanks, you guys."

"That's what friends are for," Monica said.

CHAPTER 11

Guilty

I needed invitations:

1. Fast

2. Free

3. Not cheesy

I had to give the invitations out on Thursday. Otherwise, everyone would make other plans for Saturday.

Jimmy was **my only hope** for making the invitations. That was like no hope at all, but I had to try.

I expected our talk to go like this:

Me: I need 80 party invitations. Will you make them on your computer?

Jimmy: Can you pay me?

Me: No.

Jimmy: Go away.

Our real talk went like this:

Me: I need 80 party invitations. Will you make them on your computer?

Jimmy: Can you pay me?

Me: (sigh) No.

Jimmy: (pause) Okay.

Me: (blink) Okay?

Jimmy: I'll make your invitations, but you have to let my band play at your party.

I thought I was dreaming. I pinched myself. I was awake.

My brother had a band!

I found out that:

1. Jimmy plays bass guitar.

2. Jimmy's band is called "Jimmy, James, and John."

3. They only know six songs.

4. My party will be their first gig.

I didn't even have to pay them. Jimmy said that **word—of—mouth** is the best advertising. His band wanted the whole seventh grade to hear them. Then maybe other kids would pay them to play.

That was fine with me. I was going to have a real, live band at my party.

Anna wouldn't ever top that!

* * *

The invitations looked 𝔽𝔸ℕ𝕋𝔸𝕊𝕋𝕀ℂ. Jimmy used a really cool font. The capital letters had a red outline.

The Claudia Cristina Cortez Pool Party Extravaganza

Saturday night, 6:00 to 9:00

The Harmon County Community Center

Swim! Eat! Dance!

Listen to the awesome sound of

"Jimmy, James, and John!"

* * *

I handed out the invitations on Thursday morning. By lunchtime, everyone was talking about my party.

Anna and her friends *whispered* for five minutes. Then Anna sent Sylvia over to ask what was going on. As if Anna didn't know.

"I'm having a pool party for my friends," I said. I showed **Sylvia** an invitation.

Sylvia's eyes got BIG. "You're having a real band?" she asked.

"Yeah, and they're really good," I said.

"That's so cool," Sylvia said. She gave the invitation back.

I handed it back to her. "You can come," I said. Sylvia wasn't really one of Anna's friends, and she was always nice to me.

"What about **Anna** and **Carly** and the rest of them?" Sylvia asked.

"They aren't my friends," I said.

"Oh," Sylvia said. SHE SIGHED. "Then I can't come, Claudia."

Sylvia really wanted to be **best friends** with Anna. I didn't know why. Anna IGNORED her most of the time. Still, Sylvia wouldn't do anything to make Anna mad. She left.

I squirmed in my seat. I looked down at my plate. I felt a little guilty about Sylvia.

But I was not sorry I didn't invite Anna.

Getting Even

I walked into homeroom on Friday morning. The school bully, **Jenny Pinski,** yelled, "Hey, Claudia!" Then she walked over.

I froze.

Jenny grinned. "How's it going?" she asked.

"I'm fine," I said nervously. I wondered what Jenny wanted. I didn't ask.

Jenny didn't have any real friends. **It was hard to like a bully.** But I didn't want to make her mad, so I invited her to my party.

"I can't wait to hit the pool," Jenny said. "I'm the Harmon County **cannonball champ.**"

"Cool," I said, smiling. For once, Jenny didn't seem mad at all.

"I heard Anna and her friends aren't invited," Jenny said.

"That's right," I said.

"**EXCELLENT!**" Jenny said. She gave me a **high five.** She hit my hand so hard I almost fell over.

Monica waited until Jenny sat down at her desk. Then she walked over to me. "What did Jenny want?" Monica asked.

"She's glad I didn't invite Anna," I said.

"I am, too," Monica said. "Anna has been a jerk to everyone for too long. **Somebody had to do something.**"

That's what I thought. But I felt weird, like something was wrong. I felt like **ice cream with red pepper sprinkles.** Good and awful at the same time.

* * *

I sat with my friends at lunch. My party was still **big news.** Nobody talked about anything else.

Adam sat down and shoved a slice of pizza in his mouth. When he finished chewing, he said, "Peter and Tommy want to be D.J.s too."

"D.J.s are cool," **Peter** said.

"Three D.J.s would be great," I said. "You can take turns when the band goes on break."

"How'd you get a band, Claudia?" **Brad** asked suddenly. I hadn't heard him come up behind me.

My stomach jumped, and **my cheeks turned red.** I couldn't breathe. I felt **dizzy** when I turned around.

"I know the bass player," I said.

Whoa! I talked to **Brad Turino** without stuttering! "Awesome," Brad said. He smiled. *"Save a dance for me, okay?"*

I felt like I was CHOKING. I nodded and tried not to pass out.

"Great," Brad said. "I'll see you tomorrow night."

I kept nodding, like a **Claudia bobblehead.**

After the bell rang, things got even CRAZIER.

Carly walked with me to fifth period English. "Have you written your book report yet?" she asked.

"Not yet," I said. I still had a week to finish it.

"What are you reading?" Carly asked.

I wondered why Carly wanted to know.

She only talks to me when:

1. She's making fun of me.

2. She's being mean to me.

3. She wants something from me.

"I haven't started my book yet," Carly said. "Anna's coming over tomorrow so we can read together."

"That's nice," I said.

"We're not doing anything else this weekend," Carly continued. "I guess you'll be *BUSY* with your party."

Aha! Carly wanted an invitation!

But that wasn't all. Carly doesn't do anything unless Anna says it's okay. Anna must have told her to talk to me. That meant that Anna wanted to come to my party too.

My plan to get even had worked.

I wanted Anna to know how awful it feels to be left out.

Now she knew.

So why did I feel awful too?

CHAPTER 13

Two Wrongs

Mr. Gomez stopped me on my way home from school.

"I have some **bad news,**" Mr. Gomez said. "Mrs. Gomez and I have to watch our grandkids tomorrow. We can't be chaperones at your party."

"Oh, that's okay, Mr. Gomez," I said. But it wasn't. Mom and Dad were coming, but I needed **four** chaperones.

Uncle Diego was at our house when I walked in.

"Hi, Claudia," he said.

"Hi, Uncle Diego," I said. Then I asked, "Will you be a chaperone at my party?"

"I'd like that," Uncle Diego said. "Can I go swimming?"

"Of course!" I exclaimed. "You make sure everyone follows the **pool rules.** No running, no dunking, and no cannonballs."

"What fun is that?" Uncle Diego teased.

"More fun than being splashed by Jenny Pinski," I said.

So I had **three** chaperones. I needed one more.

I went next door and knocked.

Nick opened the door and GLARED at me. "What do you want?" he asked.

"I want to talk to your mom," I said.

"Can I come to your pool party?" Nick asked.

"No," I said. Then I called out. "Mrs. Wright!"

Nick slammed the door in my face.

His mom opened it again. "Hi, Claudia!" she said.

Nick stuck his tongue out at me. I ignored him.

"Will you be a chaperone at my pool party tomorrow?" I asked.

"I'd be *delighted!*" Mrs. Wright said, smiling. Then she frowned and added, "But my husband is out of town. **I'll have to bring Nick.**"

I sighed. "Okay," I said. "Nick, you can come."

"YIPPEE!" Nick yelled. He clapped his
hands and jumped up and down. "I'm going
to Claudia's party! I'm going to Claudia's
PARTY!"

Even though seeing Nick happy made me happy, I
still didn't feel good.

* * *

Monica, Becca, and Adam brought their money to the
tree house after dinner. We had **$107 total.** I could
pay the Community Center and buy a couple of bags
of **crunchy cheese snacks**, too.

"The Cooking Club is bringing dips, cookies,
veggies, and cake," Becca said.

"That's nice," I said. I sighed.

"Cookies and cake," Monica
told me. "Not liver and onions."

"I know," I said. "Sorry. *I'm in a bad mood.*" I
couldn't get excited about food. I felt terrible.

"What's wrong?" Becca asked.

"Don't worry, Claudia. This party is going to be GREAT," Adam said.

"I bet Anna wishes she could come," Monica said.

"I know Anna wants to come," I said. "That's the problem."

"It is?" Becca asked. She looked confused.

"All of Anna's friends want to come," I said. "We should invite them. We should invite Anna, too."

My friends stared at me. Their mouths fell open.

"Wait a second. Wasn't the point to have a party and not invite Anna and her friends?" Adam asked.

"Anna didn't invite us to her party!" Monica exclaimed.

"I know, but *two wrongs don't make a right*," I said. It was weird. I thought that getting REVENGE would feel wonderful, but it felt worse than being left out.

I didn't want to be like **Anna**.

"Let's vote on it," Monica said. "All in favor of inviting Anna and her friends to Claudia's pool party, raise your hands."

All four of us raised our hands.

CHAPTER 14

Bigger, Better Bash

On Saturday morning, I took invitations to all of Anna's friends. I went to **Anna's house** last. She didn't invite me in when she opened the door. I handed her the invitation.

"What's this?" **Anna** asked.

"An **invitation** to my pool party," I explained. "It's tonight. I *hope you can come.*"

"Why would I want to come to your party?" Anna asked.

Anna makes it so hard to be nice. But I *had to do the right thing*, even if I didn't want to.

"All your friends will be there," I said. "So if you want to come, you can."

"I might. **If I don't have anything better to do**," Anna said. Then she closed the door.

I hoped Anna had something better to do.

I spent the rest of the day being nervous. My mother said that was normal. She said everything would be fine. I hoped she was right.

Most of my problems had been fixed.

1. The Community Center was paid.

2. My friends weren't mad.

3. We had tons of yummy food.

4. I had 4 chaperones.

5. I had 3 D.J.s.

6. And I had a live band.

But so many things could still go wrong.

1. What if nobody came?

2. What if everyone came and didn't have fun?

3. What if Jenny Pinski splashed everyone over and over again?

4. What if Nick peed in the pool?

5. What if Brad Turino didn't want to dance with me after all?

My stomach hurt when my parents and I walked into the Community Center at 5 p.m. But then I was too busy to worry.

My friends came early to set up. Adam, Peter, and Tommy helped Jimmy, James, and John bring in their music equipment. Then Jimmy hooked the D.J. boom box to the band's speakers. Adam's MP3s sounded AWESOME!

The Community Center staff put out coolers full of ice and soda. Becca and Monica set up the snack table.

Uncle Diego said that he would watch Nick. **Nick promised to be good.** I guess I'm the only person he doesn't listen to.

At **6 p.m.**, everything was ready.

At **6:10**, we were still waiting for the first guest.

At **6:15**, the baseball team and a dozen other kids came in.

By **6:30, half of the seventh grade was swimming.** The other half was dancing, playing Dance Dance Revolution, or just eating and hanging out.

At **7 p.m.**, Uncle Diego yelled, "*Everybody out of the pool!*"

"Why?" **Jenny Pinski** asked.

"Claudia told me you do a terrific CANNONBALL," Uncle Diego said. "Let's see it."

Jenny did her cannonball off the diving board. The splash was HUGE. Everybody cheered. Then Uncle Diego told her she couldn't do it again.

"You wouldn't want to eat soggy chips or soak the band, would you?" Uncle Diego asked.

Jenny had to think about it, but she finally agreed.

My party was saved from the Jenny Pinski tidal wave, but not from **Anna Dunlap's bad mood.**

"There aren't any hamburgers," Anna grumbled.

"It's a party, not a cook-out," Carly told her.

"But Claudia is serving cheese and crackers!" Anna exclaimed.

"It's like **a grown-up party**," Carly said.

Sylvia was impressed. "I love FANCY  food," she said.

A bunch of girls FLIRTED with Jimmy, James, and John, but I don't think anyone in the band noticed. They were too busy trying to hit the right notes.

My brother's band played the six songs they knew. Then they played them again, in a different order.

"They just played that song," Anna complained.

"I don't care," Carly said. "The bass player is so cute!"

Anna gasped. "That's **Claudia's brother!**" she said.

"So?" Carly said, giggling. "He's still cute."

My party was a hit, and Anna knew it. I had gotten even after all.

I stood behind the snack table and watched. Everyone was having fun.

"Why are you standing around, Claudia?" Becca asked. **"Go have fun."**

"I'm having fun watching everyone else have fun," I said. I smiled, but I wasn't totally happy. My party wasn't PERFECT yet.

Then **Brad** walked in the door.

"Brad!" Anna shouted and waved. "Over here!"

Brad didn't even look at Anna. **He walked right over to me.**

Brad talked. I nodded. And then we went swimming.

CHAPTER 15

P.S.

On Monday, there was an article about my party in the school paper, the *Pinecone Press*. It got **5 stars** because everybody in the seventh grade was invited. And everybody but Anna Dunlap had a great time.

The pool-and-party room did cost **$300** to rent, plus **$100** for snacks, just like Mr. Gomez told me. I found out afterward that Dad knew that was more than I could earn. **He paid the other $200** before I even talked to the Community Center.

Sylvia hired "Jimmy, James, and John" to play at her birthday party.

Nick fell asleep at 7:30. He's *mad at me* because he missed half the party. Oh well.

Brad Turino likes girls who don't mind getting their hair wet. He hung out with my friends and me all night. We swam, danced, played foosball, and ate. I didn't say much, but I laughed a lot. **We had a blast.**

About the Author

Diana G. Gallagher lives in Florida with her husband and five dogs, four cats, and a cranky parrot. Her hobbies are gardening, garage sales, and grandchildren. She has been an English equitation instructor, a professional folk musician, and an artist. However, she had aspirations to be a professional writer at the age of twelve. She has written dozens of books for kids and young adults.

About the Illustrator

Brann Garvey lives in Minneapolis, Minnesota with his wife, Keegan, and their very fat cat, Iggy. Brann graduated from Iowa State University with a bachelor of fine arts degree. He later attended the Minneapolis College of Art and Design, where he studied illustration. In his free time, Brann enjoys being with his family and friends. He brings his sketchbook everywhere he goes.

Glossary

chaperone (SHAP-ur-ohn)—a person who looks after another group of people

customer (KUHSS-tuh-mur)—a person who pays for something

deposit (di-POZ-it)—a sum of money given as the first part of a payment

dignity (DIG-nuh-tee)—sense of honor and self-respect

frantic (FRAN-tik)—wildly excited by worry or fear

humiliating (hyoo-MIL-ee-ate-ing)—if something is humiliating, it makes you feel foolish or embarrassed

maniac (MAY-nee-ak)—someone who acts crazy

receipt (ri-SEET)—a piece of paper showing that money has been paid

refreshments (ri-FRESH-muhnts)—food and drink

refundable (ri-FUND-uh-buhl)—if something is refundable, you can get your money back

rent (RENT)—to get the right to use something in exchange for payment

revenge (ri-VENJ)—action that you take to pay someone back for harm that the person has done to you or to someone that you care about

Discussion Questions

1. What are some things that make a party fun?

2. In this book, Claudia has to do jobs to make money. What do you do when you need to make some extra money? What else could Claudia have done?

3. Why did Claudia's dad pay for part of the rental fee at the Community Center?

Writing Prompts

1. Have you ever felt left out of something? Write about what happened and how you felt.

2. Write about a party that you had or went to. What was the party for? What was fun about it? What wasn't fun about it? What was the best part?

3. Are there popular kids at your school? Do you feel left out by them, are you friends with them, or are you one of them? Write about popularity.

MORE FUN
with Claudia!

Claudia Cristina Cortez

Just like every other thirteen-year-old girl, Claudia Cristina Cortez has a complicated life. Whether she's studying for the big Quiz Show, babysitting her neighbor, Nick, avoiding mean Jenny Pinski, planning the seventh-grade dance, or trying desperately to pass the swimming test at camp, Claudia goes through her complicated life with confidence, cleverness, and a serious dash of cool.

WHATEVER JOURNAL

GET LOST WITH DAVID MORTIMORE BAXTER

DAVID MORTIMORE BAXTER

Wild!

by KAREN TAYLEUR

BE BRAVE WITH DAVID MORTIMORE BAXTER

DAVID MORTIMORE BAXTER

chicken!

by KAREN TAYLEUR

THE TRUE STORY OF DAVID MORT

DAVID MORT BAX

by K

Liar!

STONE ARCH Realistic Fiction

David Mortimore Baxter

David is a great kid, but he has one big problem — he can't stop talking. These wildly humorous stories, told by David himself, will show you just how much trouble a boy and his mouth can get into, whether he's making promises to become class president or bragging that he's best friends with the world's most famous wrestler. David is fun, engaging, cool, and smart enough to realize that growing up is the biggest adventure of all.

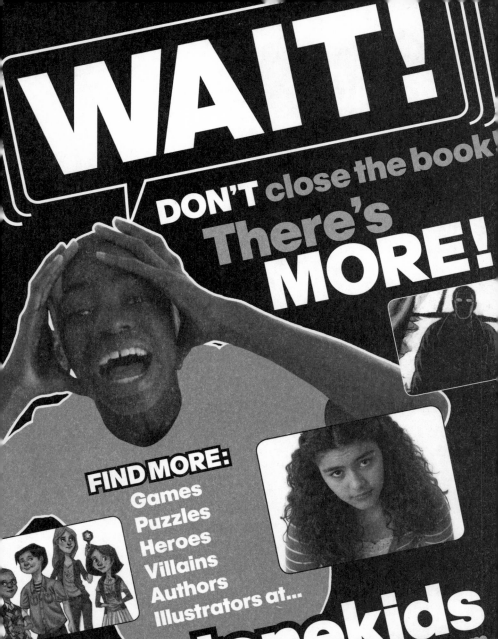